FRANNY AND THE
MUSIC GIRL

by Emily Hearn

Illustrated by Mark Thurman

SECOND
STORY
Press

For Doug

whose wit and music enliven our household

Canadian Cataloguing in Publication Data
Hearn, Emily, 1925–
Franny and the music girl
ISBN 0-929005-04-X (bound)
ISBN 0-929005-03-1 (pbk.)
I. Thurman, Mark, 1948– . II. Title.
PS8565.E22F73 1989   jC813'.54   C89-094601-9
PZ7.H32Fr 1989

Edited by Sarah Swartz, The Editorial Centre

Published by
SECOND STORY PRESS
585½ Bloor Street West
Toronto, Canada
M6G 1K5

Can you hear that dreamy clarinet?
When summer holidays began, its music floated down
from a balcony somewhere above our apartment.

I felt as if my body were dancing, dancing ... like in a
    dream.
But then, it stopped. I thought maybe my dream-maker
    was a summer visitor who had come and gone.
About that time, my daily race with the camp bus got
    totally messed up by a mysterious button pusher in our
    elevators. I'll tell you about that.

On camp mornings, I speed to beat the bus to the curb.
   And when I win, little Adam pokes out his head from
   the bus and cheers, "Way to go, Franny!"
He doesn't hear much, but can he shout!
So that whole week when the button pusher confused
   everyone and made them late, Adam bellowed,
   "Slowpoke, slowpoke, Franny is a slowpoke."
I was not pleased.

On the weekend, I decided to track down the culprit.
I turned detective and went up and down the elevators,
  endlessly ...
UP 20 floors ...
DOWN 6 ...
UP 12 ...
in hot pursuit ...
I lurked by garbage chutes ... I hid in hallways ...
I listened ... I watched....

I finally nailed her! A big scowling girl, towering over me.

I jammed my wheelchair in the door before she could get
   out of the elevator.

Nothing moved when she slammed the buttons frantically.

"What's the idea?" she demanded. "Let me out!"

I knew that if I stayed right there in the doorway Mr.
   Becks would be up to investigate.

I replied coolly, "What was the big idea – making
   everybody late all the time?"

Before she could answer, Mr. Becks arrived.

"Here's your button pusher, Mr. Becks. I've captured
   her!" I boasted, backing out.

She skinned past us both, crying, and ran down the hall.

Mr. Becks didn't follow her.
"Aren't you going to DO anything
about it?" I asked.
"Franny, now that I know it's
Maia, I have to go easy."
"EASY! All that detective work for
nothing?"

On the way down, the elevator
stopped at all the floors she'd
pushed.
This gave Mr. Becks time to tell
me something that I didn't
want to hear.
"She's a whiz on the clarinet,"
he began. My heart did a triple
flip. "But she doesn't have
anywhere to practise because
her sister is sick at home."

"Was that Maia I heard on the balcony a few weeks ago?"
  I asked.
"Yes. So many people complained that I had to stop her.
  Now she's mad at the world."
I understood that feeling, but at that moment it was just
  myself that I was mad at.
I had snitched on my dream-maker.

When I got home, I told my whole family the story.
And do you know what they said right off?
"Franny, we loved her music. She can practise in your
    room while you're at camp."
wow!

Who would tell her?
Me, of course, but how?
I settled for a note which I put under her door.

> *Maia,*
> *I love your clarinet playing and I'm truly sorry I snitched.*
> *My folks want you to practise in our place, apartment*
> *702. Please, please come.*
> *Your friend, Franny*

It worked! All summer she's been practising in my room.

On camp mornings, Adam shouts from the bus, "Where's Maia? Isn't she coming today?"

Maia sometimes joins us at camp and helps us make instruments from boxes and tin cans.

She lets us finger the keys of her clarinet, so that we can make up our own tunes while she blows into it.

And when she lets loose with her own marvelous music,
    you should see our wheelchairs dance and whirl!
Adam paints us on huge sheets of paper, splashes and
    squiggles in every colour he can mix.

When school starts again, Maia will practise there.
But she's promised to come and visit me often.
On weekends we go to the park and she teaches me how
    to play the recorder.
Yesterday my counsellor said, "Franny you're really
    making that music come alive!"
Maia smiled a wide smile when she heard that.

About the button pusher, nobody ever guessed who it was
   ... a summer visitor come and gone?

Here comes Maia. Want to hear some great music?